AaBbCcDdEeFfGgHhIiJjKkLlMmNnOoPpQqRrSsTtUuVvWwXxYyZz

Lucy & Tom's a.b.c.

SHIRLEY HUGHES

LONDON
VICTOR GOLLANCZ LTD
1986

First published in Great Britain 1984
by Victor Gollancz Ltd
14 Henrietta Street, London WC2E 8QJ
Second impression January 1985
Third impression April 1986

© Shirley Hughes 1984

British Library Cataloguing in Publication Data
Hughes, Shirley
  Lucy & Tom's a.b.c.
  I. Title
  823'.914 [J]   PZ7

ISBN 0-575-03398-3

Printed in Italy by Imago Publishing Ltd.

A Lucy and Tom know a lot of words beginning with **a**. **a** is for **a**pples and **a**nts, also for **a**pricots, **a**unties, **a**eroplanes, **a**crobats and **a**rtists. **a**

b is for **b**ooks and **b**ed. Lucy and Tom nearly always have a story read to them at bedtime. Tom knows most of his favourite stories by heart. When he's in bed he can look at the pictures and read aloud to himself. Lucy keeps some of her special books under her pillow, just in case.

B

b

C

c is for **C**ats, of course. Lucy and Tom's cat is called Mopsa. Her fur is brown with black stripes and patches of white. She doesn't often get cross or scratchy unless she's played with for just a bit too long.

c

c is for **C**olours and **C**rayons too. It's fun mixing up the colours to make different ones.

D

d is for **d**ogs. There are four living in Lucy and Tom's street. A little fluffy one, two middle-sized ones, and a big spotted one called Duchess. Tom doesn't like Duchess very much because she keeps knocking him over.

d

d is also for **d**ucks who live on the lake in the park. Lucy and Tom often take them some bits of bread in a paper-bag, and they come waddling up out of the water to be fed.

E   e

e is for **e**ggs, chocolate ones at Easter, all wrapped up in shiny paper, and real ones for breakfast. Lucy and Tom sometimes play a trick on Dad by putting an empty egg-shell upside down in his egg-cup. When he taps it, there's nothing inside. What a horrible surprise!

f is for **f**riends. Lucy's best friend is Jane. They are in the same class at school and see each other every day. Tom's friends are James and Sam. They often play together. Sometimes they get cross with each other, but friends are important people so you can't be cross for long.

F f

G g

G is for **G**ranny and **G**randpa, two other very important people.

There are plenty of interesting things to do at Granny and Grandpa's house. Lucy helps Granny in the garden and Tom helps Grandpa mend things. They have some long talks together.

H

h is for **h**omes and **h**ouses.

Can you see where Lucy and Tom live?

h

i is for **i**ll. This is Tom being ill in bed. He needs a lot of things to play with. Even then, he gets very hot and bored and keeps calling out for people to come and amuse him. Lucy is only a little bit ill. She's on the sofa, eating ice-cream.

I

i

J

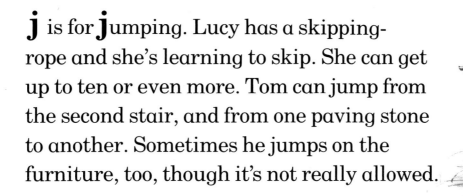

j

j is for **j**umping. Lucy has a skipping-rope and she's learning to skip. She can get up to ten or even more. Tom can jump from the second stair, and from one paving stone to another. Sometimes he jumps on the furniture, too, though it's not really allowed.

K

k is for **k**ites, flying high up over the windy hill.

k

L l

l is for **l**ight. There's sunlight, torchlight and twilight. There are street-lights, car-lights and the fairy-lights on the Christmas tree. And there's the light that shines in from the landing when Lucy and Tom are asleep.

M　　**m** is for **m**oon, the most magic light of all.　　**m**

N

n is for **n**ursery school, where Tom spends his mornings.

O

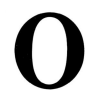

O

O is for **O**ranges and **O**range-juice, which you can suck through a straw. **O** is also for **O**ven. There are some good smells coming out of this one, but you have to be careful because it's VERY HOT.

P

p is for **p**ark and **p**laying.

p

Q

q is for **q**ueens, which is one of Lucy and Jane's favourite games. Tom is supposed to hold up their trains, but he doesn't often want to.

q

R

r is for **r**ooms. These are some of the rooms in
Lucy and Tom's house.

r

S is for **S**treets and **S**hops, Lucy and Tom have been to the supermarket with Mum. They've bought something else beginning with **S**. Can you guess what it is?

T t

t is for **t**oys, **t**eatime and **t**elevision.

U

u is for **u**mbrellas.

u

V v

v is for **V**oices. You can whisper in a very soft, tiny voice, like this, or you can shout in a VERY LOUD, NOISY VOICE, LIKE THIS, or you can make music with your voice by singing a tune. There are cross voices and kind voices, high voices and deep voices, happy voices and whiney voices. Which kind of voice do you like best?

W

w is for **W**inter when it's too cold to play outside.
The windows have frost on them and the water
is frozen over.

When the snow comes, all the world is white.

X      X

X is for **X**ylophone. Lucy's xylophone has eight notes and each one makes a different sound when you strike it. You write notes in a special way, like this:

Y

y is for **y**achts on the water and **y**achtsmen on the shore.

y

Z **z**

z is for Zoo, of course.

z is also the end of the alphabet, and
this is the end of Lucy and Tom's **a.b.c.**

AaBbCcDdEeFfGgHhIiJjKkLlMmNnOoPpQqRrSsTtUuVvWwXxYyZz